P9-BYH-067

The Story of the Little Mole who went in Search of Whodunit

The Story of the Little Mole who went in Search of Whodunit

by Werner Holzwarth & Wolf Erlbruch

Stewart, Tabori & Chang

When Little Mole poked his head out of his mole hole one day to see if the sun was shining, something very strange happened.

(It was long and brown and looked a little bit like a hot dog. Worst of all, it landed right on top of Little Mole's head.)

"Who dared to drop that on my head?" shouted Little Mole angrily.

(But, being nearsighted as he was, he couldn't see whodunit.)

Little Mole asked a pigeon who was just flying by, "Did you do this on my head?"

"Me? No, not me," answered the pigeon. "I do mine like this."

(Splattery-splosh— a wet, white blotch landed right beside Little Mole, spattering his right leg.)

Then Little Mole asked a horse who was grazing in the field, "Did you do this on my head?"

Then Little Mole asked a hare who was happily munching a carrot, "Did you do this on my head?"

Then Little Mole asked a goat who was daydreaming, "Did you do this on my head?"

"Me? No, not me, said the goat. "I do mine like this."

(Clackety-clackety-clack—shiny brown lumps fell onto the grass. Little Mole thought they looked a lot like his favorite caramels!)

Then Little Mole asked a cow who was chewing her cud, "Did you do this on my head?"

"Me? Certainly not me," said the cow. "I do mine like this."

(Swush-dup-dup—a big, flat cow pie sploshed onto the ground. Little Mole was glad that it wasn't the cow whodunit on his head!)

Then Little Mole asked a fat, pink pig, "Did you do this on my head?"

"Me? Not me," answered the pig, "I do mine like this."

(Splidgedy - splodge — a soft brown, smelly heap landed at his feet. Pee-ew! Little Mole had to hold his nose.)

Little Mole looked around for another suspect, but all he saw were two fat flies. Dining! "At long last," Little Mole thought, "I bet they can help me." "Can you tell me who did this on my head?" asked Little Mole.

"Keep still a second," buzzed the two flies, busily studying what was on top of Little Mole's head.

A moment later they shouted triumphantly, "No question about it. It was a DOG!"

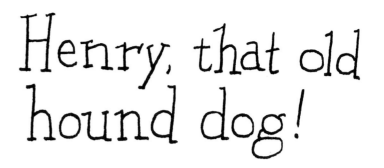

As quick as a flash Little Mole climbed on top of Henry's doghouse.

(Pling!—a little brown crescent landed slap-dab in the middle of Henry's forehead.)

The deed done, a happy and satisfied Little Mole disappeared back into his mole hole.

Library of Congress Cataloging-in-Publication Data

Holzwarth, Werner.
    [Vom kleinen Maulwurf, der wissen wollte, wer ihm auf den Kopf
gemacht hat. English]
    The story of the Little Mole who went in search of whodunit / by
Werner Holzwarth & Wolf Erlbruch.
        p.   cm.
    Summary: When Little Mole tries to find out who pooped on his
head, the other animals show him how they poop in order to prove
their innocence.
    ISBN 1-55670-348-1
    [1. Defecation—Fiction.   2. Moles (Animals)—Fiction.
3. Animals—Fiction. 4. Humorous stories.]   I. Erlbruch, Wolf.
II. Title.
PZ7.H74365St   1993
[E]—dc20
                                                    93-17676
                                                       CIP